This story is dedicated to the glory of my Savior and LORD, with the hope that others will be motivated to search God's Word for unknown heroes.

CHAPTER ONE

Psalm 9:9 "The Lord will be a stronghold for the oppressed, a stronghold in times of trouble."

Jerusalem

Sarah looked in the empty cupboard and at her husband and three boys.

Nathaniel can no longer work due to the beatings. The leaders in the temple made sure of that.

She sought help from other believers, but they had barely enough to feed their families. Some were leaving Jerusalem and heading east to Syria. They had heard Syria had gotten rain and the crops were good. She must convince Nathaniel.

But now Nathaniel's wounds needed attention. Washing away the dried blood she said, "Nathaniel, you cannot survive another beating. Your arm is broken and your ribs are bruised—just for saying Jeshua's name."

"I will heal."

"But you can't work. How will we feed our boys?"

Silence. Tears slid down his face.

He loves us, his home, his friends. But he must be realistic.

"We could take Amos's advice and leave," she said. "The boys and I could get work in the fields of Syria harvesting. Workers are needed for the harvest. Amos told us a man named Judas is quietly helping find work and shelter for other believers."

"Oh, Sarah, I'm so sorry!"

"This isn't your fault. Those from the synagogue are to blame. There's no shame in leaving. If God opens this door for us, perhaps we should go. We can find Judas in Damascus and surely he'll help us."

Silence. Nathaniel had to decide.

After a short time he said, "We will go to Damascus. The merchant Amos mentioned might help us. Let's make plans to leave. God will provide."

* * *

Dust covered Nathaniel as he winced with each step, but Damascus was in sight. The food friends had provided for the journey was gone. As they came into the city their spirits lifted. Grills frying garlic and onions with chunks of lamb filled the air with clouds of mouth-watering smells. Stomachs growling, they soon arrived at Straight Street and followed directions to the cloth shop owned by Judas.

Sarah saw the man clearly in charge, but Judas was busy with a customer. The family waited, pretending to purchase some material. When Judas finished with the sale, he approached the family. He took in the injuries of the father and the leanness of the boys and mother. They had suffered much.

"How can I help you?"

"I am Nathaniel. This is my wife, Sarah, and our three boys," Nathaniel said. "Amos ben Judah of Jerusalem told us you might help. We've traveled far . . ."

"Please, say no more. Come with me." Judas led them to the back of the shop where they could speak freely. He sent another to tend the store.

"Please, sit." He instructed a servant to bring coffee, bread and cheese.

"How is Amos?"

Following Jewish custom, they briefly discussed Amos and his family and then quieted as they consumed the needed refreshment.

"Now, Nathaniel, Sarah, what can I do for you?"

Sarah said, "We need work. The boys and I can work in the harvest. We're hard workers. Nathaniel's still recovering from terrible beatings."

"I've heard of the persecutions, the beatings. The followers of Jesus are suffering everywhere. So far, we've been untouched, but that may change."

"Judas," Nathanael added, "we don't want to jeopardize your position. Just point us in the right direction. I can't work right now, but soon I'll heal." Nathaniel could only plead for his family. His shoulders slumped and eyes averted.

"Nathaniel, there are many in your position. God's provided for them and He'll provide for you. I have an extra room at my house where you can remain as you recuperate. In the meantime, Sarah and the boys will find work. I know several men who need extra harvesters. Just today I heard of a need for a seamstress at a nearby tailor shop. Can you sew, Sarah?"

"Yes, I make all our clothes."

"Wonderful! Now, let's go to my house and get your family settled."

That evening Nathaniel and Judas were sitting near the fire. "Judas, why is all this happening? When I became a disciple of Jeshua, I thought my life would change for the better. But look how my family suffers."

"Do you remember how Jeshua told the parables of the kingdom of heaven? In one He told of a farmer who sowed good seed in his field. But while he was sleeping, his enemy sowed weeds there. When the plants came up there were weeds among the wheat. The servant wanted to pull the weeds, but the master said they shouldn't in case some wheat would be pulled. In the same way, God has left us in the midst of evil. We must grow in the midst of that evil. In the end, it will make us stronger. He said there would be tribulation, but His Spirit will never leave us."

Nathaniel considered his words. "What you say is a good reminder. My family is forever in your debt."

"When you are well and settled, you can then help others. That's how we share Jeshua's love. In the meantime, I heard Sarah say earlier you are good with numbers. I actually need someone to help me. Previously my wife, Rachel, used to keep the books for my business. She was so good at it. But she, may she rest in peace, was taken ill two years ago and passed on to be with the Lord."

"Oh, I'm so sorry. I didn't know."

"She was such a blessing."

"I do have some experience keeping books. If you'd like, I'd be happy to help."

"Wonderful. God has sent you here, I'm sure."

*   *   *

Some weeks later the sounds of children and the Sabbath celebrations filled the house.

"Nathaniel, your family sharing the Sabbath with me makes me smile," Judas said.

"It's we who are blessed. You've been so gracious to share your home."

"Since Rachel died, it's been too quiet. And now we can also celebrate the Lord's Day together. Tomorrow we can meet with other believers. I think the house will be full. We keep adding numbers each week."

"That's indeed exciting to see."

"Remember this morning when we were discussing Psalm 22 in the synagogue? Some of the elders listened when I showed how Jeshua fit the verses: 'They divide My garments among them, for My clothing they cast lots among them, My heart is like wax, it is melted within Me,' even His last words, 'My God, My God, why hast Thou forsaken Me?' I think some realized how that passage described Jeshua on the cross. We can only pray God will open their eyes to the truth."

The next day as the believers met, Nathaniel's new friend Joel came to him,

"Nathaniel, I have some good news. My cousin, who was living in the house adjacent to me, decided to return to Jerusalem. I know you've been looking for a home of your own. Would you like to live in his home? I'm sure we can work out how to pay the rent."

"A house of our own? That would be wonderful. I can't thank you enough. I'll tell Sarah right away.

Thank you, Thank you!"

Nathaniel found Sarah in the kitchen.

"Sarah, I have good news. Joel has offered to rent us his cousin's house."

"Oh, Nathaniel, a place of our own. When can we move in? How big is it? Is there a room for the boys?"

"Whoa! One thing at a time. Let's go tell Judas, and then we can go and see the house."

All too soon, Nathaniel and Sarah moved out of Judas's home. They met to worship and share meals, but Judas found his house all too quiet.

Lord, I love sharing my home. I feel that's part of my calling, especially since Rachel is gone. What am I to do now? Is there another who needs a place of refuge?

CHAPTER TWO

"Why are you persecuting Me?"

Damascus

Several nights later Judas heard a desperate knocking. He wasn't expecting anyone. He opened his door and found his friend Saul and two men, looking pale, eyes wide and searching.

"Judas, I didn't know where to go, no one else who might help me . . . Can we come in?"

"Of course, but why are you here and not with your friends at the synagogue? I heard you were coming. It's the talk all around Damascus."

"Please, just let me in. I'll explain as best I can."

"Yes, yes, come. You know the way."

"Judas, I can't see. These men have been helping

me find my way."

"What has happened? Was there an accident?"

"Please, just show my friends the way."

"Yes, yes, this way."

As Judas led them to his sitting room, the men looked around nervously. They helped Saul get seated. One of them turned to Judas. "We must go to the synagogue. They're expecting us. We'll tell them Saul is ill and is here with you."

"Certainly. He can stay with me."

The men quickly made their escape.

As Judas returned to Saul, he noticed what appeared to be scales on his eyes. "Saul, what has happened?"

"We were on the way here . . . and a very bright light suddenly appeared before us. It was so bright that it seared my eyes. Then I heard a voice saying my name, 'Saul, Saul, why are you persecuting Me?' I asked, 'Who are you?' and He answered, 'I am Jeshua, whom you are persecuting'."

"Praise, God!" Judas said.

Saul, not seeming to hear, went on, "He told me to come to the city and I would be told what to do. But I knew I couldn't go to the elders in the synagogue. They would think me crazy. I thought of you, my friend."

Oh, Saul, would you have come had you known I am a believer in Jeshua and part of the Way?

But things were beginning to make sense. Earlier in the day Judas had met his friend Ananias in the market. That morning Ananias had been praying and had a vision. He was told that he was to go the street called Straight and inquire at the house of Judas for a man of Tarsus named Saul. They knew of Saul and heard that he was on his way to Damascus to find those belonging to the Way. He was known for persecuting them and taking them to Jerusalem to go before the Sanhedrin. When Ananias left his shop, Judas wondered what to make of this vision concerning his friend. He loved Saul like a brother. They studied as young men under the Jewish teacher Gamaliel. They hadn't seen each other for some time. Now Saul was here in his house.

"Saul, I must send word to a friend. He'll know what to do."

"Who is this friend? Won't he think I'm crazy?"

"His name is Ananias. He's a good friend. I'm certain he can help."

"Ananias? I've heard that name . . . The Voice told me a man named Ananias would come and lay hands on me so that I might regain my sight, but I knew of no Ananias. How can this be?"

"God has been at work. Just trust Him." With that Judas left to find his servant and send him to Ananias.

In a short time, Judas answered another knock.

"Ananias, Saul has come. He's blind and has seen the Lord in a vision."

"You're certain that it's not a trick?"

"Come, see for yourself."

As they entered the room, there sat Saul, pale and agitated, praying. Ananias quietly approached until he was standing in front of Saul. "Saul, I am

Ananias. This morning I had a vision. The LORD who appeared to you has sent me that you may regain your sight and be filled with the Holy Spirit."

Ananias placed his hands on Saul's eyes and said, "Brother, Saul, receive your sight."

Immediately something fell away from Saul's eyes. A peace seemed to flow over him. He opened his eyes and looked at his friend.

"I can see! I now know Jeshua is the Messiah. He spoke to me on the way here. He is who He said He was—the Son of God. I must be baptized!"

Rejoicing, Judas and Ananias led Saul to a nearby pool and baptized him. As he came up out of the water he was radiant.

The men returned to Judas's house and were refreshed with olives and cheese. Ananias continued to reveal more of his vision, "The Lord also told me you are a chosen instrument to carry His name before Gentiles and kings and the sons of Israel."

It was so much for the three to take in. How could one who had persecuted the disciples of

Jeshua now be used to proclaim Him as Messiah? Only God could bring about such a thing.

For several days Saul and Judas talked, prayed, and remembered their times studying together under Gamaliel. They had often discussed the prophecies of Messiah and were now understanding how Jeshua fit them.

Saul decided to meet with the local Jews. The elders were expecting Saul, but what he shared totally caught them off guard.

"Jeshua of Nazareth fits the prophecies relating to the Messiah. He was born in Bethlehem. He grew up in Nazareth. He was in the line of King David. The portions of Psalms and the writings of Isaiah speak of His suffering and make sense since He was crucified."

The Jewish leaders were appalled. "You're supposed to be in Damascus to arrest people of The Way, and here you are proclaiming some of their blasphemies, saying Jeshua was the Son of God!"

For several days Saul kept speaking of his Savior,

angering the elders to the point they began plotting to kill him. They were even watching the city gates to prevent him from escaping.

Then one evening a group of the Jewish leaders came to Judas. "Where is Saul? We must speak with him."

"I'm sorry. He's not here. Can I give him a message?"

"Tell him to stop repeating these blasphemies in the synagogue. We'll not tolerate such talk. He must meet with us tomorrow, after the morning prayers."

"I'll pass along that message."

But Judas now knew the rumors of their plan to kill his friend were true. That night Judas and several others of the Way met Saul.

"Saul, the elders are planning to capture you tomorrow after the morning prayers. You must leave tonight."

"But how can I escape? The gates are guarded."

"We have a plan. Joel ben Judah has a home along the north wall of the city. One of his windows looks out beyond the city. If we put you in a basket, we can let you down beyond the city wall. You'll not have to pass through a gate."

"He's willing to risk this?"

"Yes, he's also a believer in Jeshua. He's happy to help you."

Later Judas and several men let Saul down over the wall and provided supplies of blankets and food for his journey. Saul said farewell and headed for the Arabian Desert.

Over the next several months Saul, now known as Paul, returned secretly to Damascus to talk with Judas. He was overwhelmed with guilt for all the believers he had persecuted and caused to die.

"How can God use me knowing all I've done? I watched while Stephen was stoned. I brought many to Jerusalem for the same fate."

"Paul, what does David tell us about God in the Psalms? 'Thou, O Lord, art a God merciful and gracious, slow to anger and abounding in steadfast love and faithfulness.' And later he repeats in many

Psalms that the Lord is merciful and gracious, abounding in steadfast love."

"But I have persecuted so many and denied Him so long . . . "

"That's true, but the prophet Joel tells us, 'Yet even now . . . return to me with all your heart, with fasting, with weeping, and with mourning; and rend your hearts and not your garments.' Dear friend, I have seen you do this. You've confessed your sin and repented as John also told us. And God is abounding in love and forgiveness and forgives your sin. He'll not hold it against you."

"I hear you, but—"

"There is no BUT. You have repented and believed in Jeshua's sacrifice for your sin. You are no longer under the Law. You are under God's grace."

Paul was quiet, thinking about his friend's words. "You are right, Judas. Thank you. During my time in the desert, God also reminded me His timing is perfect. He revealed Himself to me when He chose.

And His grace is sufficient to cover all my sins—and indeed I have many. I'll pray and consider your wise words, Judas. You're a good friend."

Over the next few days, as the two friends talked, Paul decided it was time to go to the disciples in Jerusalem. Judas prayed with him as he prepared to leave.

However, in just a couple of weeks, Paul returned to Damascus. The visit to Jerusalem had not gone well. The disciples were not totally convinced of the change in him.

"I think it's time for me to return to Tarsus. I've heard there are some of The Way there. The disciples distrusted me, all but Barnabus. I think God's closed that door right now. But I feel drawn to Tarsus."

"Then go there, Paul. I know God will use you, wherever He leads you."

"I'll send word as often as I can. I believe God's also using you, Judas, to minister to believers in need. You've helped me so much and encouraged me with God's truths. Keep sharing His truth."

"I will. Keep in touch. I'll be anxious to see what God has planned for you."

Chapter Three

Psalm 56:3 "When I am afraid I put my trust in Thee."

Jerusalem

Leah was preparing the noon meal when Orpah appeared at the window. She held up a package. Leah knew it was a new bed cover she had ordered. The Moabite tailor was known for his beautiful material. He often sent Orpah to deliver his merchandise. Leah always enjoyed talking with her, but today Orpah appeared distressed, diverting her eyes, her head slightly bowed.

Now as she entered the kitchen Leah could see she had been crying.

"What's wrong, Orpah? Why the tears?"

"Oh, Leah. You've been so good to me. You encouraged me when I heard Peter speak of Jeshua and trusted Him as my Savior. And then when my parents disowned me and sent me away, you took me in and found me work with the tailor. But now the tailor is selling me. He says it's all he can do. Times are hard. He's not making enough money to keep me as his servant. He's selling me to Felix, a Roman soldier. Leah, he is old. He's known for his drinking and parties. I've heard he is cruel. What can I do?"

"Oh, Orpah, I'm so sorry. What can I do? I feel like I got you into this mess."

"There's nothing. He comes for me today. I only wanted you to know, to ask you to pray. I know Jeshua goes with me, but I'm afraid."

Leah grabbed her hand. "Lord, we don't understand what's happening, but we know You are faithful. You've promised to always be with us. We pray Orpah will be a light in this darkness. Help her to share Your love and grace. Give her Your peace in this difficult time. Amen."

"Amen. Thank you, Leah. I won't forget your kindness."

"Oh, Orpah . . . " Leah hugged her tightly.

Chapter Four

Psalm 37:23 "The steps of a man are from the Lord, and He establishes him in whose way He delights."

Damascus

It was Passover. Judas was preparing to travel to Jerusalem. For him it meant loading his damask material and following the usual trade route from Damascus to the Holy City.

How I miss Rachel. She always made the trip so enjoyable.

The journey would be long, but the Romans had soldiers all along the route providing a safe passage for the desired goods from the East.

Rachel and I always felt safe traveling this road

to Jerusalem. This time Nathaniel's traveling with me. He'll make sure a proper accounting is made along the way. His skill with numbers fills a need in my business. And Nathaniel's boys are joining us, their first trip back to Jerusalem.

At the outskirts of Jerusalem, they set up camp and made their way to the temple. They joined the throngs anticipating the special celebration. However, for Judas and Nathaniel there was the added excitement of meeting with other followers of Jeshua and celebrating the resurrection of their Beloved Savior.

They celebrated the Passover meal at the house of Judas's friends, Amos and Leah. Solemnly, Amos, following Jeshua's example, went from guest to guest washing the other believers' feet. When he finished, Leah and some other women served the meal. Everyone remembered the last Passover Jeshua had with His disciples.

Judas said, "When He had given thanks, He broke the bread and said, 'This is My body which is broken for you. Do this in remembrance of Me.' In the same way, He also took the cup after supper saying, 'This cup is the new covenant in My blood. Do this, as often as you drink it, in remembrance of Me.' For as often as you eat this bread and drink this cup, you proclaim the Lord's death until He comes again."

The promise in Jeshua's words brought smiles to the otherwise solemn occasion.

The believers rejoiced over the next few days, remembering the empty tomb and Jeshua's resurrection. Mary, Jeshua's mother, retold stories of His appearing to many disciples and followers.

The only damper to their joy came when some told of the numbers being persecuted.

"I'm sorry to report that the beatings continue, some by other Jews and some by Roman soldiers seeking slaves or fearing a revolution. Some families are torn apart and children made orphans. I'm reminded of what our Lord said, 'Allow the children to come to Me.' We need to consider how to help these families, especially the children. Judas, do you have any ideas?"

"They need a woman's touch. I'll ask families as we travel back to Damascus if any are willing or able to help. Perhaps we can find homes for some. I'll let you know."

"That would be great."

"So, Amos, what do you know of Paul? I haven't heard from him in quite a while."

"Paul spent some time in Tarsus and then began to journey to other parts of the Roman Empire. He was last sharing with those in Prisidian Antioch."

"I knew God had a special plan for him. Oh, how God is using Paul. All the way to Galatia."

"Indeed, we love hearing of so many coming to faith in Jeshua."

"Well, it's been a long day. Thank you for your hospitality, Amos. Come, Nathaniel, we must prepare to travel in the next two days."

Chapter Five

Psalm 47:6 "The Lord lifts up the downtrodden."

Jerusalem

The Passover meal and sharing with friends ended. Leah was watering plants in her garden when a woman appeared at her gate. Her face hidden by a shawl, she wore the bright colors of a prostitute. When she called out, Leah immediately recognized the voice of Orpah.

"Oh, Orpah, what's happened? Come inside."

Orpah was thin and walked slightly bent over. "Who's done this to you?"

Through tears Orpah told how Felix often had drinking parties with other Roman soldiers, would dress her up and offer her to his friends. "When I refused or fought back, I was beaten and forced to do unspeakable things. I cannot continue with such shame, so I came to you, Leah, my only friend."

Leah immediately drew her close and let her cry. When she had quieted, Leah said, "I know of a believer friend, Judas, who is in Jerusalem on business and to celebrate the Passover. Perhaps he can help us."

* * *

That night Leah sent Orpah to the entrance of Judas's tent. Nervously fingering her shawl, Orpah requested to speak with Judas. It was unusual for a woman to come at night, but Judas sensed that quiet Voice that spoke peace to his soul. He asked her to come and sit, but she remained standing, looking only at her feet.

"Please, what is it you need?"

After several silent moments she said, "Amos's wife Leah sent me. She said you might help."

"Tell me what you need."

"My master sold me to Felix, a Roman soldier. This man is known for his parties. I'm only a slave and am forced to do what he requires."

Judas could read between the words she spoke. "If Leah fears for your life, I'm also concerned. Come, my servant will hide you until I've spoken with Felix."

Judas knew Felix. He was a greedy man. He had an idea and went to pay him a visit the next morning.

Felix was surprised to see the Jewish visitor appear at his home. Few Jews came to a Roman's house, but Judas was a well-known merchant. Perhaps he came to sell him something.

Judas got right to the point. "I understand you have a servant girl named Orpah. I would like to purchase her service. I'm in need of more help in Damascus."

Felix's eyes opened wide. *What a surprise. This Jew wants to buy my worthless, pitiful slave.* "Well, she's quite valuable to me. You would need to pay me well for such a gem."

Disgusted but holding his emotions in check Judas said, "I'm willing to pay a fair price, but surely you've other servants that do more than she. She appears quite weak."

"No, no, she is not weak." *She's only pitifully lazy and obstinate.* "I'm sure she'd be an asset for you."

"Name a price."

After much dickering, they settled on a price.

When Judas returned to his tent he called for Orpah.

"Orpah, you're free now. I've paid Felix for your service and you are free to go."

"Oh, thank you, thank you. How can I repay you?"

"Consider it a gift. But Leah tells me you worked for a tailor and can sew. I might be able to give you work in my cloth shop in Damascus. Would you be willing to go there?"

"Oh, yes. That would be an answer to prayer."

"Then come with us. We leave in the morning."

Orpah, given her freedom, eagerly joined Judas and his caravan. On the journey, Judas met with other believers along the way asking if any could take in orphans. So far only one family promised to get word to Amos in Jerusalem.

Lord, what is to be done about these orphans? I am only one man. And yet, I know You are faithful.

That night the caravan stopped along the Jordan River where the Jabbock River connects. The Roman soldiers in this area were familiar with Judas and his beautiful materials. One commander, Longinus, approached.

"Judas, I see you're returning from Jerusalem. How is business?"

"Good. God blesses me on each trip."

"May I look? I want to buy some material for my wife. I need to buy her favor. My company is moving out in a few days, so we'll have to move, again. She hates moving."

"Where are you headed?"

"We're being assigned to Caesarea Philippi, but

my troops may be called out as far as Damascus. That's your town, isn't it?"

"Yes, my shop is in Damascus. You must come there if you're sent to Damascus. May I ask, why are they moving you there?"

"Apparently some rebels have been threatening there. Jews all over this area are causing problems."

"Longinus, I know of no rebellion, and I have business with many Jews. In fact, I myself am a Jew by birth, but I've joined those of The Way who follow after Jeshua who was crucified."

"I've heard of the Way. Most seem to be peace-loving, but some officers fear their loyalty is not to Caesar but to another king."

"Longinus, we were told by Jeshua, our Messiah, to render unto Caesar what is his and unto God what is His. Jeshua's kingdom is not of this world and is no threat to Caesar."

"That may be so, but be careful. Times are changing. I fear honest men like you will be caught in the crossfire."

"Thanks for the warning. So, what can I show you for your wife?"

The next day as Judas and Nathaniel packed up to leave, they discussed Longinus's words and the changes the Roman troops were making.

"Judas, why do they fear us? The Lord never said He'd overthrow Caesar. He taught us to love one another and show kindness and mercy to all."

"Yes, but there are those who don't want Rome to rule over us. They're promoting rebellion, and that makes the soldiers wary. Only time will tell how this will end. We have to trust that God has a plan. Enough talk of soldiers and rebellion. I've discovered that Orpah is skilled with a needle. She was servant to a tailor in Jerusalem. I was thinking. Making a tailor shop next to the cloth store might be a smart idea. God brings two women to me who can sew, and for what purpose? Maybe a tailor shop. What do you think?"

"I think that's a great idea. Why, you've space right next door to add on. The boys and I could build it. I think it'd work."

*   *   *

Within a month, Nathaniel and his boys had added a tailor's room to the side of Judas's shop. Nathaniel's wounds were healing and Sarah joined Judas as plans progressed to open the tailor shop. She and Orpah were organizing their new work place.

"Orpah, I'm so glad God has brought you here. It'll be so good to work with you."

"Are you sure?" She looked away. "I've done many bad things. Will your husband and boys not be offended?"

"We know you were forced to do those things. God forgives you. We can do no less. Come, let's sort these needles and threads and prepare for our first customers."

Chapter Six

Psalm 16:1 "Preserve me, oh God, for in Thee I take refuge."

Rome

Dori paced from the kitchen to the sitting room of her palatial home.

Where is Alexander? I sent the boys to bed hours ago, but Alexander hasn't returned. He said the meeting would be late, but this is very late. What could've happened? The followers of Jeshua are being careful. We've seen friends being sent to the Colosseum and never returning. Oh, why did they have to meet tonight?

A quiet knock interrupted Dori's thought. Opening the door, she saw Alexander's friend Julius.

"Dori, you and the boys are in danger. Alexander was taken by the Roman guards this evening. They'll be coming here next for you and the boys. You must leave at once."

"What happened?"

"We were praying for the men and women who were taken last Wednesday. But as we were getting ready to leave, ten soldiers entered the house and began grabbing us. I managed to get out the back before they grabbed me, but I saw Alexander being tied up with four others and led away. When they find out who he is, they'll come after you and the boys. You must leave now."

"But where can we go?"

"There's a safe house on the outskirts of Rome. We've prepared this place for such a need. I'll take you there. Gather what you can carry and bring the boys at once. I don't know how much time we have."

Traveling at night they approached a small cottage. Dori could see the safe house was in a vineyard.

"Lydia and Gaius own this vineyard. They'll keep you safe until you decide what to do."

"But I can't leave Alexander."

"For now, just rest here. I'll send word to you soon."

Julius knocked, made swift introductions and left.

"Dori, you and your boys come with me. Our basement is a good hiding place. I'm sorry you'll have to remain hidden. Soldiers often come here to purchase wine, so you must not be seen."

"Gaius, we don't want to bring you trouble."

"It'll be no trouble. We, Lydia and I, have hidden others. You'll be safe."

"I fear for my husband, Alexander. If he's taken to the Colosseum, what will become of him?"

Lydia put her arms around Dori. "We'll pray for Alexander and the others that were taken."

It was two weeks before any word came. Lydia and Gaius slowly came downstairs to speak with Dori and her boys. "Dori, word has come just now.

I'm so sorry. Alexander and the others were seen in the Colosseum yesterday. The lions were set on them. They had no escape."

Dori's wail was heart-wrenching. "What am I to do? I have nothing. My boys have no father. I have no husband."

Lydia let her cry. Gaius talked with the boys, trying to console them.

The next day Gaius approached Dori.

"I'm so sorry to rush you. I know your sorrow is great. But you must make some decisions soon. Claudius has told all Jews and Christians to leave Rome or face the consequences. I know of others who are leaving and going to Corinth. They know of your loss and are willing to let you travel with them. There's a couple, Aquila and Priscilla, who will help you. But you must leave tomorrow. They are kind and believers in Jeshua."

Dori's felt her only choice was to make the journey to Corinth with Priscilla and Aquila, the tent-makers. *As Abraham and Sarah were told by*

God to leave and go to a land they did not know, I must also go. But, Lord, it is so hard.

* * *

The next morning Dori and her sons, Jesse and Hosea, awoke early.

"Come on boys. We're going on an adventure. We're going to a faraway place."

"But what about Father?"

"Oh, Hosea, you know he's now with the Lord. Gaius told you what happened in the Colosseum."

"But, I miss him."

"I know, but I know he'd tell you to go on this new adventure. We'll see many new places. Come now, Gaius is waiting."

Gaius led the family to the edge of the vineyard and there stood a young couple. Priscilla immediately came to Dori.

"Oh, Dori, we're so sorry for your loss. But we're so glad you're joining us. We also felt it was time to leave Rome."

"I am Aquila. We're blessed to have you travel with us. And these fine boys must be Jesse and Hosea."

Their shy smiles reassured Dori this was the right decision.

So the journey began. They arrived in Corinth and Aquila explained where they were going.

"This port city that connects Rome to the East is a commercial trade center. Its history dates back many centuries. Corinth was known for ship building, bronze, and pottery. In 146 B.C. invading armies had destroyed the city, but in 44 B.C, Julius Caesar ordered the city rebuilt. The city soon became a melting pot of people from many nations, and merchants flocked here. Now, of course, there are also gamblers betting on the Isthmian games, prostitutes and many fleeing Rome as we are.

"Farmland, vineyards and olive groves encircle the city, but most of the daily business is conducted in the marble-paved "agore," or marketplace. This is where we're headed."

They set up shop in a vacant building near a local synagogue. In no time they had a daily routine.

Dori rose early and prepared a morning meal while Aquila and Priscilla began sewing on the orders for tents that came flowing in. Dori cleaned house and made sure the boys continued their studies in the Torah. Fortunately, Dori had always studied the Scriptures with Alexander in Rome and could now help her boys. Aquila often led further discussions as they sat around their evening meal.

"Priscilla, you and Aquila have been so generous to allow us to stay with you."

"Nonsense, Dori, we're the ones blessed. I'd never be able to manage helping Aquila with the tents and keeping house. And you know I can't cook. I even burned the last Sabbath loaves. You're such a good cook. Look at the pounds we've gained since eating your tasty meals."

"Your protection of my family means so much."

"We love being 'Auntie' and 'Uncle' for Hosea

and Jesse. They bring us much joy."

* * *

Sometime later Aquila came in breathless. "Priscilla, Dori, we'll have a guest this evening. Another tent-maker has come to Corinth. And guess what? He's also a teacher, sharing the stories of Jeshua as he travels. He's recently come from Athens, but I hear he caused quite a stir there and in Thessalonica. His name is Paul. I asked him to join us. I'd like to invite him to stay with us, if you think we can squeeze one more into our home."

"Yes, oh yes. A teacher of Jeshua!"

Dori easily provided meals for one more. Paul worked as a tent-maker part of the time and spent the rest of his time arguing in the synagogue every Sabbath and persuading some Jews and Greeks to believe in the Messiah.

Dori was preparing an evening meal as Paul, Aquila, and Priscilla came from the shop. Hosea, five, and Jesse, seven, immediately jumped up to greet the three adults.

Dori smiled.

The boys are happy again. Paul and Aquila always take time to lift up each boy and swing them over their heads and onto their shoulders. Thank you, Lord, for giving them father-figures who are willing to both teach them and provide for them.

Some days later Silas and Timothy, two of Paul's friends, joined them. The house couldn't hold the three men so they moved to another house near the synagogue, the home of Titius Justus. God continued to bless their work and many joined the group of believers.

However, after several months, Paul became restless and began to discuss moving to a new location. "Every time I go to the acropolis and look out over the water, I think of Ephesus. I feel drawn to it. I think God is leading me to move on. I've spoken to Silas and Timothy and they wish to remain and continue teaching the new believers. What about you, Aquila?"

"We'd go with you. We're anxious to reach out with the message of Jeshua. We'd be willing to go to Ephesus. Let's ask Dori if she's also willing to go. She's been such a big help."

Dori's response was quick. "Of course, I'm happy to go with you. Seeing God work here and touch so many lives has been a blessing. Why, there's now a church filled with young believers. How exciting that is to see. Perhaps God wants this for Ephesus also."

"I believe He does," Aquila said. "So, Dori, Priscilla, let's pack up and go with Paul."

The group set sail for Ephesus. Aquila and Priscilla were very excited to minister to believers there. Again the tentmakers set up shop, but in no time Paul was determined to go on to Syria. Now Dori had to make another decision.

"Dori, Paul needs help if he plans to travel on to Syria. He certainly would be grateful for your assistance. But of course, we, Aquila and I, would love for you to stay here with us. You've become like family, and we'd miss you and the boys terribly. You need to decide. We're praying that you'll make the right decision. We'll abide by whatever you choose to do."

That night Dori sought the Lord.

"Lord, I love Priscilla and Aquila. They're like family for me and the boys. But, I can't explain it. I'm drawn to Syria also. I've never even been there, but I feel You're asking me to go with Paul. Why Syria? I can't even imagine. What do you have for me, Lord?" As she prayed, peace surrounded her, not knowing why, but trusting God had opened this door for her.

The next morning Paul was saying goodbyes to the believers and promising to return, if God was willing. At the side door he saw Dori and her boys with bags for traveling. He knew this was a big decision for her, but she seemed intent on going to Syria.

So they set sail for Caesarea, spent some time in

Antioch, and then departed for Galatia and Syria. Paul ministered to the believers along the way and finally headed to see his friend Judas in Damascus.

Chapter Seven

Isaiah 55:9 "For as the heavens are higher than the earth, so are My ways higher than your ways, and My thoughts higher than your thoughts."

Damascus

As Damascus came into view Dori thought,

What am I doing coming to a strange city where I know no one. Lord, did I not hear You correctly? What have I done? Who will help me? I have no husband, and Paul will not stay here. What was I thinking?

Paul approached a shop and walked quickly as a man came into view.

"Paul, what are you doing here? I didn't know you were coming. Come inside out of the sun."

Then Judas noticed the young woman and two small boys standing nervously off to the side.

"Paul, have you a wife?"

"No, no, this is Dori. Dori, come and meet my friend Judas. These are her two boys, Hosea and Jesse. They've been helping me as I travel. Dori is an excellent cook, and she's a believer. She agreed to journey with me here. But, enough, do you have room for these weary travelers?"

Flustered at the appearance of a family arriving with Paul, "Of course, where are my manners? Come, we'll go to my home right away and get you settled. What a long journey you've had. The last I heard you were in Corinth, Paul."

"Yes, we left there, traveled to Ephesus where Aquila and his wife and I taught. I left them there, wanting to make my way back here. Actually, I won't be staying long. I want to make my way back to Ephesus, but I wanted to check with you and the believers along the way."

"Well, come, we'll get all of you settled."

Dori and her boys were led to a guest room with two beds. They placed their meager belongings in cabinets and Dori headed to the kitchen. As she entered she saw two women preparing an evening meal. One was older, and the younger looked so much like her she must be her daughter.

"Good evening. I am Dori. My two boys are Hosea and Jesse. We're Judas's guests."

"Blessings, I am Naomi and this is my daughter Martha. Welcome."

Dori saw a pile of dirty dishes and moved toward the tub of water to wash them.

"No, no! You are a guest. We'll do those later."

"But I want to help. I can't just sit and do nothing. That would be taking advantage of Judas's hospitality. He's been gracious to let us stay here."

"Oh, Judas and Paul are great friends. He'll be happy to have you here."

"So, you've been with Judas's household a long time?"

"Oh my, yes. We came here when Rachel, his

wife, was still alive. My husband died of cholera and left me and Martha with no family and nowhere to go. Since Rachel died, Judas has been so sad. He works hard all day, but at night it gets so quiet. He doesn't complain, but I hear him sigh and pace. He misses her. Judas is a good man. It'll be good to have Paul here and you with your boys."

"Well, you can be sure it won't be very quiet anymore with two boys running around. But I was concerned we would impose."

"Oh no. He and Rachel were always taking in travelers—some they knew and some were strangers that became friends. They both loved the Lord and felt God had blessed them with this large home so they could offer refuge for others."

"Well, it's certainly a blessing for me and my boys."

"Dori, may I ask, what happened to your husband?"

"He was killed in the Roman Colosseum, for his faith."

"I'm so sorry. So, are you and Paul going to marry?"

"Oh my, no! I've been helping him travel. I've cooked for him when he's stopped to share about Jeshua. When he said he was coming to Damascus, I said I'd go with him."

"Well, we're glad you've come. The meal is ready, so let's serve it."

Dori was surprised when they all gathered together for the meal. Judas treated his servants just like his guests as they sat together for their meal. Judas thanked God for the meal and friends to share it with, and then they all enjoyed the food.

Later that evening Paul and Judas sat by the fire catching up with what they'd been doing since their last meeting. Paul explained, "Dori's husband was killed in the Colosseum in Rome, and so Priscilla and Aquila took her with them when they fled to Corinth. She ministered to them and me for many months, and Dori agreed to journey with me here.

"It's a dangerous time, Judas. Jews are being sent

from Rome. Christians, those of the Way, are beaten and ostracized by the Jews. When we came through Caesarea we heard more tales of believers being questioned and beaten by Roman soldiers who thought they were rebelling against Rome. There are many children who've lost their parents and just roam the streets."

Judas nodded. "We've also heard these reports. But we're far enough from Rome to remain out of the worst of it. Many more here are coming to know the Messiah as Lord. The believers will be anxious to hear you teach. But what of Dori and her boys? Is she going to travel with you? That must be difficult with the boys being so young."

"She's a strong woman and a loving mother. She loves the Lord and wants to serve Him, no matter where she is. She's been a caring servant to me. I'm just not sure what she plans to do now. She felt God was leading her here. But I'm not sure how that will work, a widow with two boys."

"That's an amazing story, for a woman to travel

so far, trusting God to provide. That kind of faith is rare. I've heard of many widows and orphans who are struggling to survive."

"Yes, indeed."

"Does she have any family?"

"My understanding is her parents died of some disease. Her husband, as I mentioned, was killed and I know of no other family. That's why Aquila and Priscilla took her along with them."

Judas got very quiet.

What are you doing, Lord? Yes, I've been lonely in this quiet house since Nathaniel and his family moved. Orpah is staying with them, too. But I cannot have a woman with children just move into my home. Yes, she is a widow with orphans, and You've told us to provide for them. But how will that look? What would You have me do?

"Judas, what is it? You've not heard a word I've said."

"Oh, sorry, I was just thinking. Why did you bring Dori to me?"

"I don't know, it just seemed like the right thing to do. You've always taken in those in need. God knows, you certainly helped me when I needed it. And I know you've helped others. I guess I just thought you'd know what to do."

"I'm not sure . . . I'll need to pray about this."

"Don't worry, Judas. I'm not leaving right away. You'll come up with something. Now, tell me about your business. You seem to be doing well."

They spent time catching up. Paul related how many Jews were believing in Jeshua as Messiah, even Gentiles.

"Judas, it's amazing how God has touched even some prominent Romans with the truth of Messiah. You remember the disciple, Luke, who was a doctor? Well, he has a friend in Antioch who has become a believer. He used to be a Roman general, but since his conversion he's been relieved of duty and gone into hiding. I hope to visit him when I leave. He's so eager to learn. I also hear that Luke has written down, in order, details of the life of

Jeshua so Gentiles and others who want to know
more of God's promises will have His life recorded
to read and study."

Judas listened but was unsettled and found it hard
to concentrate on what Paul was saying. He was
pleased to hear news of new believers, but the next
several weeks were going to be life-changing, he
could feel it deep within.

*   *   *

Dori decided that if she was going to stay in this
house, she must find a way to help. After talking
with Judas's cook, she began to help with the
household immediately. Because of her servant
attitude, Judas's servants were accepting of this new
arrival and recognized her loving and caring spirit.

Judas watched as she began to fit into the daily
routine. He saw the change in his household, and he
no longer felt so lonely.

She is certainly a woman of God. She has an

inner beauty, as well as an outer beauty. She obviously loves her boys and has such a servant-attitude. And yet she seems to almost lead the others in a gentle way.

The weeks passed quickly. Paul was again feeling God direct him to continue his journey. Judas asked to speak to him privately. A nervous Judas greeted Paul.

"Paul, I want to ask your advice about something."

"Sure, is it a theological question? A question of Scripture?"

"No, it's a more personal issue."

By now Paul could see Judas perspiring and even his hands were shaking. And then he realized Judas knew he was leaving soon and the issue of what to do about Dori and the boys was before him.

Paul leaned back and smiled. "You care for her, don't you."

"Who, what . . . ?"

"Dori, and the boys. You care for her. I see she's

become a part of your household, an important part."

Judas sighed. "Yes, she has."

"What are you going to do, my nervous friend?"

"What do you think of the custom of kinsman redeemer? Like Boaz and Ruth?"

"Judas, you're not her kinsman. But you can ask her to marry you. I've seen how happy she is. Her boys love it here. Just ask her."

"But do you think she'd agree? What if she says no?"

"Ask her."

Just then Dori entered carrying a tray of snacks. With an innocent yet knowing look she spoke, "Ask her what?"

Judas knew then he had not hidden his growing love and concern for Dori.

"I need to ask if she would marry me."

"And I believe she would say, 'Yes.' "

Paul delayed leaving to be a part of the wedding.

"Judas, Dori, God has brought you two together for a glorious purpose. He who began a good work in you will bring it to completion. I can leave knowing God will continue to use you both."

*   *   *

In the next few months the tailor shop filled with customers. The cloth shop could barely hold the number of people looking for goods.

"God is blessing us for a reason, Judas. Look at all these people!"

"He is, Dori. I believe God's moving. I just wish I knew what He wants me to do."

"Perhaps as we travel to Jerusalem for the Passover, He'll make that clear."

"We'll ask Him to do just that. As David said, 'My times are in His hands.' "

Chapter Eight

Psalm 68:5-6 "Father of the fatherless and protector of the widows is God in His holy habitation. God gives the desolate a home to dwell in."

Jerusalem

"The journey to Jerusalem is easier with you by my side, Dori."

"The boys and I are blessed to be under your loving care, Judas. God has been good to us."

"Indeed."

But the journey presented some unexpected challenges.

"Judas, look at the people leaving Jerusalem. They look so tired and hungry. Look, there are even children. Those three over there don't seem to be with anyone. Please, let's stop here for the night."

They chose a camping spot, and then Dori slowly approached the children who seemed to be traveling together. The oldest boy put the others behind him as Dori came close.

"Hello, children. Where are you headed?"

"We're going north to Galilee. Why do you want to know?"

"Where are your parents? We'd love to meet them."

They looked around, obviously hesitant to answer.

"It's okay. We were just wondering if your family would want to share our evening meal. We're just now stopping to rest for the night."

Dori looked behind her as Judas came up.

"Yes, we'd be honored if your family joined us. Dori is a very good cook."

"I think our parents have gone on ahead, but we might be able to stop for a meal."

"So, it's settled. Dori will prepare a meal and you can meet our two boys, Jesse and Hosea. They'd love to have some company."

As Dori and the boys moved away, Judas saw a Roman soldier nearby frowning. Judas went to him.

"Do you know where those children's parents might be? They seem to be alone."

"I've been watching them and seen no adults with them. In fact, I'm thinking they might steal from other travelers and are up to no good. I'd watch them."

"Thanks, sir. We will."

As Judas returned to their camp, he found the children already playing. Dori was preparing some lentil soup over the fire.

"What did the soldier say?"

"He never saw their parents. Thought the boys might be thieves."

"Oh Judas, God has put them in our path. We must gain their trust and find out who they are."

"Let's feed them and give them shelter for the

night. Perhaps in the morning we can find out more."

The next morning as Dori was preparing their meal, the older boy came to her.

"Thank you for feeding us and giving us a place to sleep."

"No problem. It was our pleasure. We'd love to help you if we can."

The boy looked away.

"Your boy Jesse said you're on your way to Jerusalem. What will you do there?"

"We're going to the temple for Passover, and then we'll meet with friends. We come each year, when we can, to celebrate. We'd love to have you join us."

"Jesse said you were of the Way. Is that true?"

Dori was surprised Jesse had shared that. They didn't tell many, but Jesse must have had his reasons. "Yes, do you know about the Way?"

"Yes, our parents were also believers in Jeshua, but . . . "

"Oh, dear boy, what are the tears? Are your parents part of the Way?"

"They were . . . They were taken by some soldiers. Many have been taken and accused of sedition and then executed. We've not seen them for weeks and have nowhere to go. We stayed with some other families, but they hardly have enough food for themselves."

"Oh, I'm so sorry. Please, come with us to Jerusalem. You'll be safe with us. There are some guards who know us and will warn us of trouble. Here's Judas. Judas, tell him."

"Actually, Dori and I talked last night. We assumed you were on your own. And if your parents are really gone, we'd love for you to come with us back to Damascus, that is if you want to."

"That would be wonderful. I don't know what to do with my sister and brother. They are so young and afraid. But you don't even know our names."

"True, but you can easily fix that. What are your names?"

"I am Matthew. My brother is Simeon, and my sister is Naomi. Are you sure?"

"All good Jewish names. Welcome, Matthew, Simeon and Naomi. You've met our boys, Jesse and Hosea. I am Judas, and this is my wife Dori. We would be honored to have you travel with us. So, it's decided. You'll stay with us and be a part of our family."

Jesse and Hosea, standing nearby, had been quiet up to that point, but hearing this they jumped up and hugged Matthew and Simeon. Dori bent down and welcomed Naomi who smiled shyly.

"Come, Matthew, Jesse. You can help me load up. I can use extra help."

That evening, settled with friends in Jerusalem, Dori and Judas spoke with Amos and Leah about the children.

"Amos, Matthew told us their parents were believers and taken away by Roman soldiers. Can this be true?"

"Yes, many are being rounded up with accusations of sedition. And then they just disappear. Some return in a few days, but some are never seen again. I'm afraid his parents have been killed."

"Well, we're taking the children with us to Damascus. I can't imagine how they've suffered."

"How wonderful of you to take them in. Is there anything we can do?"

"Just pray that the transition for the children will go smoothly."

"Oh, they're already connecting with your boys. God's certainly put you all together."

The time in Jerusalem went quickly, and soon the family was packing to leave.

"God bless all of you as you journey home again. Grace and peace to you."

"Thank you, Amos. You've been so good to let us stay with you here. Please be careful. We'll be praying for you here in Jerusalem. There's so much unrest."

"And I'll add my prayers for you both, Leah, Amos. God's grace and peace to you."

*   *   *

The return trip home went smoothly, but Judas was concerned about the future.

"Dori, where are our children going to sleep? Have you figured that out?"

"Not a problem. The four boys can share a room. We may have to make bunk beds so that they'll all fit in one room. But Naomi will have to take a guest room. I think it'll work just fine."

"I'll get Nathaniel and his boys to help with the beds. Our family has grown quickly. But I'm so glad we stopped when we saw those children. I weep for those we didn't see. God always tells us to care for the orphans, but I think we may not always see the need."

"Judas, God will open our eyes to things He wants us to do. If there are more children in need, He'll show us. For now, we have these three. And what a blessing that they are already believers."

"Dori, I need to tell you what Amos shared with me. Rome has sent word to the soldiers in Jerusalem to silence the rebellion. They're ordered to round up any Christians who call Jeshua their king. For now, we in Damascus are safe, but things are changing quickly."

"When my boys and I lived in Rome, the believers there had a safe house, away from the city, but ready for any who needed to escape. Maybe we should find such a place."

"You're right, and I know just the place. My family has some property on the Arabana River, about twelve miles from Damascus. There's a small cabin there, but I haven't been there in years. It's beyond the Roman controlled lands. It would make a safe place if needed."

"What are you thinking?"

"I think Nathaniel and I will soon make another trip. We'll have to add on to the cabin, and we might need room for others."

"But Judas, if it's out of Rome's jurisdiction and roads, how will we get food and supplies?"

"Let's take one step at a time. First, let's see what the cabin and property look like now. No one has lived there for many years, but I know it's on the river, so we'd have water and the possibility of irrigation for crops. I'll speak with Nathaniel tomorrow."

In just a few days Judas and Nathaniel collected supplies for their trip.

"Nathaniel, do we have all the tools and wood you'll need if we add on to the cabin?"

"I collected what we'll need, but won't the soldiers along the way question us?"

"I know many of the men. I plan to tell them I'm building another shop in a nearby town. When we take the path north, we'll soon be out of their jurisdiction and no one'll be on that less traveled path. However, it'll be a rough journey. There are no Roman-built roads there."

"That sounds ideal, no soldiers."

"I believe God's provided just the place for us to have a safe house. Remember what Solomon wrote? 'Many are the plans in the mind of a man, but it is the purpose of the Lord that will be established.' "

* * *

Time passed quickly. Dori and Sarah worked hard at the cloth and tailor shops. The children helped however they could.

"Dori, they've been gone a month now. When do you think they'll return?"

"Should be soon, Sarah. I know Judas wanted to prepare the place in case we're threatened."

"I hope it's soon. I miss Nathaniel."

"In the meantime, we need to be thinking about supplies we'll need if we have to leave here. I'm thinking material for clothes, bedding, seeds for planting. What else?"

"Cooking pots. Dishes. Do you think we'll really have to leave Damascus?"

"God will show us. Until then we'll just be prepared."

* * *

Judas and Nathaniel could see the houses of Damascus as they came over the hill.

"I'll be glad to see Sarah and the boys. I've missed them."

"We've accomplished a lot. At least now there's shelter for our families if needed. The land was better than I remembered. Trees for building, open land near the river for planting crops. Room for children to play. My concern is for the children's education. We can certainly teach them what we know, but it won't be like the teachers they have now in Damascus. But, God knows our needs. He'll provide."

"Besides, we don't have to leave Damascus just yet. It's still safe for us. Your friend, Longinus, will warn us if there's danger."

"You're right. Since he became a believer, he's a dear friend and brother. I remember the day he came to my shop. I thought he wanted to buy some material, but what he really wanted was answers . . . "

"Ever since I came to Damascus I've been watching the Jews and Christians for signs of insurrection, but all I see is love and caring for one another, and even toward me, a Roman soldier."

"We are taught to love one another by Jeshua."

"But look, you have even taken in orphans and made them part of your family. I've not seen that kind of love anywhere."

"God loves those children and asks us to love them too. We could do no less."

"So, tell me more about Jeshua."

"And that's how Longinus chose to follow our Lord. He's always asking questions and learning. He's become a dear friend. Ah, come, our families are in sight!"

Chapter Nine

Acts 13:47 "I have set you to be a light for the Gentiles, that you may bring salvation to the uttermost parts of the earth."

Ephesus

The day began just like any other. Except now he was running for his life.

Andrew was hiding behind one of the stalls in the busy Ephesus market, listening for the angry voices pursuing him. Shouts echoed around him as he tried to cover himself in the midst of straw and dung that had been left for the pack animals. As the voices retreated to another section of the market, Andrew peeked to see if anyone was around. Seeing no one, he decided to move to another location.

What am I going to do? Where can I go?

The market seemed quiet, so Andrew ventured down the lane where vegetables were sold. He needed to avoid the booths of the silversmiths.

Why have they singled out me? Why did they think I was hurting their sales? Yes, I've spoken out in the hall of Tyrannus, as well as Paul, about worshipping idols and following Jeshua, but why have the silversmiths gotten so mad?

As he made his way through the market, he found the street where Paul had taken up residence with Aquila and Priscilla. *Perhaps they could help him figure out what to do next.*

Andrew found the gate, entered and saw Priscilla weeding the garden.

"Shalom, Priscilla. Is Aquila or Paul here?"

"They're inside. Come."

"Andrew, we were just praying for you. Come, sit."

"How did you know I needed prayer? I was just running from Demetrius and his friends. I think they're blaming me for the loss of business selling those shrines of Artemis."

"Yes, when Paul was at the hall he heard they were looking for you and him. Paul made his way back but didn't know where you were. I'm glad you made it here safely."

"Andrew, Aquila and I've been asking God what to do. We believe God is telling us to send you to a safer place. You and I've been vocal and persuasive, teaching from the Scriptures, turning a considerable number of people to be disciples of Jeshua. We've convinced many that gods made with hands aren't gods at all. But this has enraged many. I'm preparing to leave for Macedonia. I believe my time here is completed. But you . . . I think God has another path for you."

"What do you mean, another path?"

"Would you consider going to Damascus? Paul knows of a believer there who could help you get settled. And there's a group of believers that could benefit from your teaching."

"I haven't considered this before. Who is this friend?"

"My friend's name is Judas. He's already helped many who are fleeing persecution. I know he'd help you."

"Damascus." *Lord, is this where I should go? How would I get there?*

His thoughts were interrupted by Aquila. "There's a caravan leaving tomorrow for the east. I'm certain you could travel safely with them."

"Okay, I'll go to Judas in Damascus, God willing. Perhaps God will use me there."

* * *

The caravan was a mixture of merchants, soldiers, and travelers. There were few Jews traveling with the group, and they would've been upset with the talk and language used by most. But Andrew tried to mingle with them. He saw this as an opportunity to share his faith.

One evening by the campfire someone mentioned how beautiful the night was, with stars so bright and numerous. Andrew joined the conversation.

"They are so beautiful. God has given us a lovely evening to enjoy."

A soldier responded, "What god do you refer to?"

"I refer to the God who made the world and everything in it, being Lord of heaven and earth."

"And what is the name of this god?"

"He is Elohim, Almighty God. He doesn't live in shrines made by man, nor is he served by human hands. He made every nation of men to live on all the face of the earth, that they should seek God and find Him. He's not far from each of us for the Scriptures say, 'In Him we live and move and have our being.' "

"But what does this god look like?"

"He's not made of gold or silver or stone, a representation of the imagination of man. *He* is the Creator, Who existed before the foundation of the world."

"I'd like to hear more of this god of yours. As we travel you can tell us more. But for tonight, I must get some rest. We leave early in the morning."

"What is your name, soldier?"

"Julius," he said and he turned away.

Lord, what door have you opened? A Roman soldier that wants to hear more of You? Give me your words to say.

Over the next several days, Andrew shared with Julius. But they too quickly arrived in Damascus.

Lord, the seeds have been planted in this searching man. Reveal Yourself to him as only You can.

* * *

Andrew found his way to the cloth shop on Straight Street, and there he found Judas.

"Aquila, Priscilla and Paul send you greetings."

"Oh, please, come in and tell me of Paul and his friends."

"Paul is well. He was in Ephesus and saw many miracles. God used him mightily. Some whom he taught even burned their books on magic. It was amazing! But others fought against him and me, so he's traveling to Macedonia. Aquila and his wife are remaining in Ephesus, but they're being used by God to touch many lives."

"It's good to know where Paul is. We can pray for him and his journey. Now, what can I do for you? Are you in need of work?"

"Paul thought I might be able to teach and minister to the believers here. Of course, I'll need some work and a place to stay. I don't want to be a burden to anyone."

"So, what work have you done in the past?"

"I've done many things: construction, carpentry, even selling vegetables in the market. I'm willing to do whatever is needed. But most of all, I love to teach."

"I'm sure you'll find work here. In the meantime, you can stay in our guest room until you're settled."

"Thank you, Judas. I was told you'd help. You're most generous."

"There's a believer in the area who is building a new shop in the market, one street over from here. I'll check with him and see if he needs help. And a teacher for our children is something we've been praying for. I believe God sent you here for a purpose, so He'll provide all that's needed."

By the next day Andrew was working at the building site with the merchant, Josiah. Josiah told Andrew he could stay at the site each night. He would have shelter and Josiah would have a guard for his building. During his free time Andrew was able to share the Scriptures with believers. They met every Sabbath, and he told stories of Jeshua and the work that Paul and others were doing to spread the Gospel. Every evening he collected the children together to hear lessons from the Holy Scriptures.

"Tell us of Goliath and David again!"

"Well, how tall was David, do you remember?"

"Maybe like Jesse?"

"Maybe. And how tall was Goliath?"

Several shouted, "Like that olive tree!"

"Yes, but why was David not afraid?"

Naomi shyly lifted her hand, "He knew God would give him extra power when he threw that stone at Goliath."

"You are so right, Naomi! And that's what God does for us. He helps us stand up against those who would hurt us. And like David, God shows us how to do what is right."

"So, should we throw rocks at the Roman soldiers?"

"No, Matthew. Jesus taught us to love our enemies and pray for them. You've seen how we've been kind to Longinus and other soldiers, and because of that they now love the Lord. Goliath, on the other hand, was demanding that someone battle with him. David was the only one willing to defend the people and face the enemy. He didn't start the fight."

"But the Roman soldiers have killed many of us!

Shouldn't we defend ourselves?"

"Matthew, you're correct. Many of you have lost family. But the rebels and zealots are the ones who cause much of the problem. They forget the Lord's command to bless those who persecute you, live in harmony with one another, repay no one evil for evil, for God says, 'Vengeance is Mine.' So, as hard as it is, we must try to overcome evil with good."

The children got very quiet.

This is a hard lesson, Lord, for these who've lost loved ones. Only You can comfort them and heal their pain.

Chapter Ten

Psalm 3:8 "Deliverance belongs to the Lord; Thy blessing be upon Thy people."

Damascus

News from Jerusalem was not good. Travelers with the caravans told of food shortages in the cities, especially among the Way. As Judas watched from his shop, a familiar couple slowly approached.

"Amos! Leah! I can't believe my eyes. You're in Damascus. Oh, come inside. You look so weary."

"Thank you, Judas. It's been a long journey."

"Please, sit, have some refreshment. Then you can tell me what's happened."

As a servant brought some food Amos began, "Things are changing in Jerusalem. We who are of the Way are shunned by the Jews and harassed by the soldiers. Leah's garden was destroyed, dug up and scattered. Our gate was torn down. At night rocks were thrown at the house. It was time to leave. I feared for our lives. We had to get away."

"I'm so glad you came."

"We don't want to burden you. We hoped you could give us advice, direction."

"For now, you'll stay with us. Our home is a bit crowded, but we can always fit in more. Just last week two more orphaned girls were added to our family. Dori is amazing with the children."

"But put us to work. We don't expect to do nothing."

"Dori will be thrilled to have Leah's help. And I can always use an extra hand. Come, let's get you settled."

* * *

In no time Amos and Judas became a team, and

Dori and Leah had the household running smoothly. Then one afternoon Longinus appeared at the shop.

"Longinus, welcome. What brings you here at this time of day? Why aren't you with your men?"

"Judas, we've gotten word that Rome is burning, and Nero blames the Christians. Many are being killed, and of course many are fleeing. We're told to be on the lookout for what Nero calls 'dangerous' Christians."

"He blames the Christians for the fire?"

"Yes, but many say he may be responsible. He's used Christians as torches to light the city. He's despicable."

"Be careful, Longinus. Now that you've taken Jeshua as your Savior, you too may be in danger. If others know you're a believer and talk like this . . . "

"I'll be careful, but you are well known. If the order comes down for us to roundup Jews and Christians, your family will be in danger."

"Thanks for the warning. We'll keep watch."

"Peace and grace to you."

"And to you also."

*   *   *

That evening Judas, Nathaniel, Andrew, and Amos discussed the recent events in Rome. Already more travelers were seen on the road through Damascus.

"Judas, perhaps we need to consider more preparations for our safe house. Our numbers have grown. We'll need more rooms."

"You're right, Nathaniel. Amos, would you be willing to go with Nathaniel and a couple of the boys to our place on the river? I think we need to start moving supplies there and add on to the living quarters."

"Of course, whatever needs to be done."

"I'd go also."

"Andrew, we need you here to keep the children busy with their studies. I think more time spent studying at home will be better than being seen at the synagogue. It'll also give some order to their lives. Things may drastically change soon."

"Of course, whatever you think."

"Now, let's let Dori, Leah and Sarah know to start collecting supplies to take to—what shall we call it? The Refuge? The Garden?"

"*The Garden* is good. It won't sound suspicious when we speak of it." All nodded their approval.

"*The Garden* it is!"

Chapter Eleven

Psalm 61:1-3 "Hear my cry, oh God, listen to my prayer...Lead me to the rock that is higher than I; for Thou art my refuge, a strong tower against the enemy."

Damascus

The preparations of the Garden came together. Nathaniel and Amos returned, having added more living areas: one for Leah and Amos, one for Nathaniel and Sarah, and three for others who might come in the future. They decided to all share cooking and meals together in one large room, and the children were to sleep in either the girls' or boys' sleeping rooms which they enlarged. They even managed to mark out a large garden area near the river for irrigation.

The next Sabbath the believers came together and were praying: requests for the sick to be healed, safety for those traveling, peace for those suffering persecution. Then Longinus stood.

"We need to pray for the Jews and believers here in Damascus. I've just heard that due to the zealots' revolt in Jerusalem, an order is sent out to round up all Jews and Christians."

"And what's the purpose?" one asked.

"I can't say for certain, but it can't be for good. Nero's sent his son, Vespasian, to quell the rebellion in Judea."

"When is this to take place?"

"I think within a few days. No official word has come, only rumors."

"Thank you, Longinus. This will be a matter for consideration and prayer. We're so blessed to have you." Turning to the group Judas continued, "God has warned us. Now it's up to us to listen and heed what He says."

Andrew added, "Remember what Jeshua told us, 'Do not be anxious how or what you are to answer or what you are to say,' and I believe He would add, 'what you are to do' . . . for the Holy Spirit will teach you in that very hour."

They spent some time praying and then quietly left for their homes.

As soon as Judas, Nathaniel, Andrew and Amos returned to Judas's home for their meal, the discussion began.

"Judas, I feel God's saying to get our families to the Garden."

"I agree, Nathaniel. What about you, Amos? Do you agree?"

"Oh yes, it's time. But won't we rouse suspicion if we all just pack up and leave?"

"You're right. Perhaps Andrew could take the women and children for a 'field trip' to learn about planting crops in the spring. Actually, the timing is perfect. We may need to actually do some planting at the Garden if we're going to relocate there."

"I can take them. But maybe Nathaniel should come also, to help with the loading, unloading, and organizing."

As the women came in to serve their meal, Dori added, "We're ready, Judas. Leah and I've planned for this day. It'll only take a day to load our supplies and be ready to leave."

"Wonderful! Amos and I will follow soon."

The next day the men loaded the supplies on wagons for a 'field trip' with the children. Judas and Amos sent them on their way with, "Have a fun trip!"

"See you when you get back."

"Tell us all about what you learn when you return."

With the families on their way, Judas and Amos had to decide how to leave the business. Much would be lost, but there was no choice. One sewing machine and spindle and lots of needles, thread and material had been taken to the Garden already, but much had to be left behind.

As they discussed details, Longinus appeared wide-eyed and pale.

"The order has come. All Jews and Christians are to assemble in the town plaza two days from now for a census. But I'm certain counting is not the purpose. Your lives are in great danger."

"We're ready, Longinus. We'll say we're going to Jerusalem to buy supplies. We go often, so there shouldn't be a problem. We're in your debt again, my friend. Please be careful."

"Leave soon. I think you can make it to the road north out of our jurisdiction before the troops arrive. They are in Caesarea Philippi collecting the Jews and Christians but will head here next."

"You can join us, Longinus."

"Not now. But I'll keep your offer in mind. God speed. You'll be in my prayers."

"Blessings and peace to you also."

*   *   *

The next morning Judas and Amos had their wagon loaded, looking very much like merchants going to market. They left at dawn. The road seemed to be busier than usual. Familiar, yet serious-looking soldiers nodded as they passed by the city gates.

"I've done business with these soldiers for years, Amos. Now God's given us favor with them."

Just a couple miles out of the city, two soldiers approached. Judas immediately recognized Longinus but didn't know the other frowning man.

"Good morning. Longinus, is that you? You've not been to my shop to buy for your wife recently. I hope all is well."

"Who is this man, captain?"

"He's a businessman in Damascus, general. I often buy beautiful damask material from him."

"What are you doing on this road today?" the impatient general asked.

"We're on our way for trading and buying supplies. We're always in need of something. I'm so glad the Roman soldiers are keeping this busy highway safe from thieves. We're in your debt."

"Humph! Well, be on your way. We want to clear this road for other soldiers who're going to Damascus tomorrow."

"Thank you, general. Good to see you Longinus. Come to my shop again soon."

Judas moved the ox team ahead, not looking back, but very aware of eyes following them.

"I'm so glad Longinus was with him. I don't think it would've gone so well otherwise."

"You're right. The general seemed to be less abrupt when he said he knew us."

They moved on toward their turn. "Judas, look at these families. The women and children seem to be wearing more clothes than needed for the weather today. I think word has gotten out about the Jewish 'census.' Many are traveling today."

"I think you're right. I'll be glad when we reach our road. 'When I'm afraid, I will trust in Thee.' David's words keep running through my head."

Hours later Judas whispered, "There's the path.

Let's stop and check our load. I want to wait for some of these travelers to get out of sight before we leave the main road."

As a family approached, Judas recognized the familiar friend Josiah and his family.

"Judas, Amos. You also took Longinus's warning seriously."

"Yes, it seemed our only choice. But where are you headed?" Judas asked.

"We're going to family near Caesarea Philippi."

Amos said, "We just met Longinus and a general who are clearing that road for soldiers. You'll be stopped."

"We've nowhere else to go. We need to check on our family there."

"Please, come with us," Judas said, "We can make room for you. Then when things settle down, you can go and check on your family. But right now, it's not safe."

Josiah and his wife quietly exchanged words.

"We were afraid to go there but saw no other

option. If you're sure, we'll join you. We have goods and supplies we can share."

"Of course, but let's move from here before others come," Judas said.

The road was empty as far as they could see, so Judas turned the oxen onto the dirt path that led to the Garden and safety. Josiah and his wife followed.

As Judas and Amos approached the Garden, the children jumped up and down and Dori and Leah ran to meet them.

"Oh, Judas, you're safe! We were so worried. We've been on our knees praying for you," Dori said.

"We're here. We're fine. Come. We're hungry and tired, but praise God, we made it safely. Josiah and his wife have joined us also."

Dori looked at Josiah and his wife. "Welcome. We always have room for more. Come, we'll get you settled."

Nathaniel and the boys unloaded the wagon while the women served Judas and Amos a meal. When they were all settled together in the shared living area, Judas began.

"Longinus came to us soon after you left. He'd gotten word that Nero had sent troops, headed by Vespasian, to round up Jews and Christians for a 'census.' But he believes they'll all be killed. So, we left this morning. As we were leaving, Longinus and another gruff soldier stopped us with many questions. Thanks to our friend and the good Lord, things went smoothly and they let us pass."

"How blessed we are to have a friend in Longinus," Leah said. "But I'm afraid for him. It's dangerous for him being a believer in Jeshua."

"He'll be careful. But I know he's worried about the census, gathering up the Jews and Christians all in one area. He's afraid many will die, and he doesn't want to be a part of it," Amos said.

"We need to pray for him," Dori said.

"Yes. Dori, why don't you lead us," Judas replied. "And we'll pray for all those left in Damascus. You know, on the road, after we turned off the main

Roman road, God reminded me of some words Isaiah wrote, 'Though the mountains be shaken and the hills be removed, yet My unfailing love for you will not be shaken nor My covenant of peace be removed.' I know God has given me this peace. I think we need to pray peace for those who are in Damascus and this 'census day.' They and their families will need *God's* peace."

And so the couples prayed for those left behind and thanked God for the Garden He had provided.

Chapter Twelve

Micah 6:8 "He has shown you, oh man, what is good; and what does the Lord require of you but to do justice, and to love mercy, and to walk humbly with your God."

In the Garden

The vegetable garden was growing. Everyone worked, weeding, planting seedlings, and watering. All were busy in the field when two suspicious travelers approached. The man wore dust-covered clothes and his robe was torn in places. His head was covered, so his face couldn't be seen. The woman was nervous and wore clothes too large for her size.

Judas was immediately on alert and moved to meet the man before they entered the property. As he came closer the man spoke, "Judas, I need your help!"

Judas immediately recognized the voice. "Longinus, what are you doing here? What has happened?"

"I couldn't stay, Judas. It was horrid. Those defenseless people. All killed."

"Come. Let's get some water and food and you can tell us what's happened."

As all the men gathered in the common room, Dori and the women prepared some refreshment, listening to the conversation.

"I've deserted. If I'm found I'll be killed, but I couldn't be a part of the massacre."

"Start from the beginning," Judas said.

"Well, you saw me on the road with that officer. He reported directly to Vespasian. The soldiers arrived and on the appointed day all the Jews and Christians were led, some forcefully, to the plaza. Then with no warning or explanation the soldiers began the slaughter. Only those who fled earlier or were in hiding escaped. I couldn't bear it and slipped away. I found these rags to wear and smeared dust all over us. As we fled Damascus we were stopped by some soldiers. But since I was a Roman and not a Jew, they let us go. I cannot be part of that. No life is sacred to them. How can God forgive being part of that?"

"God knows your heart, my friend. David wrote a psalm that tells us, 'He who dwells in the shelter of the Most High, who abides in the shadow of the Almighty (that is you, that is me) will say to the LORD, my refuge and my fortress. And when he calls to Me (that is God), I will answer him; I will be with him in trouble, I will rescue him and honor him.' You've chosen to follow the Almighty and acknowledge Jeshua died to take your sin. You're not responsible for the actions of these soldiers. Indeed, I believe God is pleased with your choice to leave, and I think God knows we need someone to provide security for us. Who better than you?"

Andrew added, "David also wrote we're not to

fret because of the wicked but trust in the LORD and do good. We're just glad you're safe with us."

"Longinus, go wash and change into the clothes Dori has collected. You and your wife are part of us now. By God's grace we've been spared this evil, and somehow God will use for good what was meant for evil."

*   *   *

Just as Longinus told them, some Jews and Christians fled before the plaza slaughter. Over the next several weeks refugees arrived at Judas's community. Some were goat herders, some carpenters, weavers, cooks and gardeners.

"God is growing our community, Dori. Look at how He has saved so many believers."

"Yes, at last count we're nearly one hundred. God spared many, and we know some have fled to other places."

"Isn't God amazing? His Word is spreading, even

as the Romans try to eliminate it."

"I wonder what comes next?"

*   *   *

The community continued to grow and thrive. The seasons came and went as the believers praised God for the peaceful place He provided.

But change and challenges were coming. As new people arrived, news came of the fighting continuing in Jerusalem and the death of Paul in Rome.

"Dori, my dear friend has gone home. I remember him saying, 'For me to live is Christ, and to die is gain.' He was hard pressed choosing to live or die, for to be with Christ is far better than life here. Now instead of being held a prisoner, he is safe with the Lord. But he'll be missed."

Chapter Thirteen

Psalm 37:23 "The steps of a man are from the LORD, and He establishes him in whose way He delights."

The Garden

Dori, Judas, Jesse and Hosea walked along the river and selected a shady spot for their picnic. The family was on a much-needed outing. As the boys collected firewood, Dori and Judas sat listening to the gurgling stream.

"Look how the boys have grown, Judas. They're no longer children. Hosea has his eye on Miriam every chance he gets. He'll want to marry soon. And Jesse. He loves studying the Scriptures with Andrew and reads and rereads Paul's letters to the churches at Corinth."

"They've become fine young men who seek the LORD with all their hearts. God has truly blessed us. Having our community of believers makes us all stronger. I think it's time to allow Hosea and Jesse to have more of a leadership role. Here they come. Now seems like a good time to discuss it."

"Here we are. Found lots of branches for our campfire. Jesse even found a couple big logs. See?"

"You did well," Judas said.

"Isn't the river peaceful. The quiet Voice of God is easy to hear in a place like this."

"So true, Jesse. And what does that quiet Voice tell you?"

"That He'll never leave us or forsake us. That He'll always be our refuge."

"And what do you hear, Hosea?"

"That He is in control and not to fear—but, I also hear my growling stomach that says it's time to eat!"

"Okay, okay. Let's ask a blessing and have some lunch. Your mom has prepared a feast, as usual."

After finishing lunch Judas said, "Jesse, Hosea, I want to discuss something with you."

"What is it?" Jesse asked.

"Is anything wrong?" Hosea added.

"No, no. Quite the opposite. You boys have grown up to be godly men. You're a blessing to me and your mother. You're also a blessing to our community. You know the Scriptures, you hear God's Voice, you have compassion for those with needs. I think it's time for you both to take on more of a leadership role in our community."

"But, you are our elder. You and Amos and Nathaniel are wonderful leaders," Jesse said.

"Yes, for now. But eventually, as Paul prepared Timothy to take over his role, I must also consider who will fill my position when the time comes."

"Hosea should be the one to take your place. He is the oldest. He even wants to settle down and raise a family here. But, I, I feel God is leading me differently."

"Jesse, what do you mean, differently?"

"You know Jeshua said to go into all the world, preach the gospel, baptizing and teaching them to observe all that He taught. I want to go . . . into all the world, to all the churches and preach and teach. Andrew and I have talked some about this already. He has told me how he used to travel to the churches."

All were quiet. Jesse looked out toward the river west. Finally Judas asked, "How long have you felt this calling?"

"For a long time, maybe since we first arrived in Damascus."

"Jesse," Dori said quietly, "I remember how you so easily connected with Matthew and his siblings when we went to Jerusalem and found them. You've a heart for others in need and aren't afraid to share your faith."

"Mother, I love you. It's been hard to make this known because I don't want to hurt you. It would mean leaving you and the others. But I know it's what I should do."

"Then you must do it. If God is calling you to this, your answer can only be, 'Here I am LORD, send me.' "

Jesse hugged his mother and looked over at Judas. Tears were in his eyes.

"You've blessed your mother and I—even as we shed tears of both joy and sorrow, sorrow thinking of you leaving, but joy that you seek to do God's will. We'll bring this before the elders when we meet again. For now, I think I could use a hike with my family."

Chapter Fourteen

Psalm 37:39 "The salvation of the righteous is from the LORD; He is their refuge in the time of trouble."

The Garden

Eventually news came of the Romans subduing Jerusalem. Jews were distraught and fleeing.

Judas had just come from the garden when Longinus called to him, "Judas, there are several people, maybe three families, approaching on the other side of the river. I think we need to go and speak with them. They don't look dangerous but very weary."

"Okay, let me call Jesse, too."

The three crossed the river and met up with the

haggard group. Judas spoke first, "Shalom. Where are you headed? Can we be of help?"

The elder of the group answered, "We're former citizens of Jerusalem. But we had to flee the Roman soldiers. You sound kind, but that tall one with you looks like a Roman."

"Friend, we are a peaceful community who all worship the One true God and His Son Jeshua. We'd be most happy to offer you rest."

"But we are Jews who do not follow Your Messiah."

"No matter. We're most of us Jews by birth. We welcome you. Your families, your children, look weary and in need of food and rest. Please. Let us help."

"I am Gideon. Our families provided sheep for the temple sacrifices. Now the soldiers killed most of our sheep, so we've no work. We had to flee."

"Come, Gideon. We have food and shelter for your families. You've suffered enough."

Longinus and Jesse helped carry some of the

children who could barely walk. As they crossed the river and entered the Garden, the refugees looked around, amazed at the abundance of food and stock they saw. Dori and the other women prepared a feast for their hungry guests. Little was said as the group ate hungrily. Then after moving some supplies to the common area, the three families were led to a storage building where Nathaniel and several men and boys were quickly constructing small sleeping rooms. The building wasn't fancy, but it would provide shelter and some privacy for the newcomers. The women brought them some bedding and left them to settle into their new quarters.

That evening the believers met in the common room for a meal and worship. They praised God for their protection and provision. Then Judas led a discussion of how to proceed with their new guests.

"I believe God has sent these needy families to us. We can offer them shelter and food, but it will be up to them if they wish to remain with us."

One of the young men questioned, "But they're

not followers of Jeshua."

"True, but I don't believe Jeshua would have us turn them away. 'If you minister to the least of these my brethren, you have ministered unto Me.' "

Jesse spoke up, "Jerusalem is being destroyed and they're hurt, confused, and searching for answers. We have those answers."

"Well said, Jesse. For now, we just need to love them, give them a safe place and let God open their hearts to hear His truth. This is God's work."

And so, the community agreed to allow the families to remain for as long as they wanted.

* * *

All of the refugees seemed to revive, except for one young boy. His condition seemed to worsen. Gideon, his father came to Judas.

"Judas, my son Jacob is ill. Is there anything you or someone in your group can do?"

"Actually, if you agree, I'll call our elders to pray

for your son."

"I, I'm not sure."

"Gideon, we'll pray and ask God to intervene. Then it'll be in God's hands."

"Okay, I'd be grateful."

Judas called Nathaniel, Amos, Andrew, Hosea, and Jesse to pray. As they laid hands on Jacob, Jesse prayed, "Lord, You've said where two or three are gathered, there You are in their midst. You alone have the power to heal, so we ask, in the name of Jeshua, that You touch Jacob and heal him."

The men anointed him with oil and continued to pray silently.

The next morning Gideon and Jacob came to the meeting room for breakfast.

"Look, Judas, Jacob is much better! I think your prayers helped," Gideon said.

"Praise God. He has healed your son. Let's thank Him right now."

After giving thanks, Gideon could not keep quiet. "Please, I want to learn more of Jeshua. The elders in Jerusalem said He was a rebel and a fake. What can you tell me?"

Judas said, "Let's have breakfast and then you can join us as we study the Scriptures. Then you can decide for yourself if He is a fake or not."

The families with Gideon joined the community as they looked at the readings that came from Genesis, Leviticus, and even Isaiah.

Judas began, "God from the beginning of creation in the garden has wanted to dwell with man. But then when Adam and Eve sinned, tried to be like God, our Holy God removed them from His Presence. But Leviticus shows us He still desired to dwell with man and thus had them build the tabernacle, a place to meet God. Isaiah also reminds us that God continued to want to meet with man and so the temple was built and animal sacrifices made to remove man's sin.

"But God wasn't finished. He'd promised in Genesis and the prophets that one day a Messiah, Savior, would come. That Messiah was God, coming as a man, as Jeshua. He was the final sacrifice. Isaiah spoke of His suffering, and we know Jeshua died on the cross. But more than that, we know He rose from the dead. He appeared to many after that, and He was alive! But then, as He returned to heaven He sent His Spirit to dwell with us. Dwelling with us was always God's intention. And now if any man is willing to acknowledge Him as Messiah, he can have God's Spirit living in him."

"Wow! You've given us much to think about. But I want to hear more," Gideon said.

So, Gideon and his family looked at the prophecies of Messiah and how Jeshua met each requirement.

Judas said, "Gideon, do you see how the temple sacrifices foreshadowed the Lord's ultimate sacrifice? Even the prophet Samuel wrote, 'Has the LORD as great delight in burnt offerings and sacrifices, as in obeying the Voice of the LORD? Behold, to obey is better than sacrifice, and to listen than the fat of rams.' "

"That's amazing! I've helped with the temple sacrifices all these years and never realized the significance."

Eventually Gideon and his family came to the elders.

"We're convinced. Jeshua is the promised Messiah. He was our sacrifice for all time and we want to be baptized."

"We're so happy for you and so thankful God has opened your eyes to His truth. Come, we'll baptize all of you in the river."

Chapter Fifteen

Psalm 119:105 "Thy word is a lamp unto my feet and a light unto my path."

Near the Garden

It was morning and Judas was praying. A movement across the river caught his eye. He could make out a large man walking purposely toward the Garden. Judas rose, alert to the possible danger. But that quiet Voice within only spoke peace to his heart. He waited until the man reached the bank and called, "Are you lost, friend?"

"I was lost but now am found, was blind but now I see. Grace and peace to you. I am Theophilus of Antioch. I'm looking for Judas of Damascus."

Judas hurried to the river's edge. "Please, come. I

am Judas."

As they arrived at the community building, several of the men and women joined them to hear what the new arrival could tell them. Judas made introductions.

"This is Theophilus. His name means 'Lover of God.' Paul often spoke of him in Antioch. We're honored to have you."

"Please, the honor is mine. I've heard much about you, Judas, and am blessed to see so many here in your community. So many Christians have been killed and many brutally treated. But I've good news and sad news."

"Please, share what you know. We're so isolated. It's hard to keep up," Jesse said.

"First, I must tell you, our dear brother Paul has gone to be with the Lord."

"His death saddened us all, Theophilus, but we did know this. He was my dear friend."

"I'm sorry for your loss. But this next news may be a comfort. Luke, my dear friend, has sent me a long letter, a book really, that chronicles how God has used Paul and others to share the good news throughout the world. And that's what I've brought to share with you."

Everyone started speaking at once and asking questions.

"Whoa! One at a time!" Judas called out. "Theophilus will answer our questions, but let's not all ask at once. First, how long can you stay with us? We obviously have many questions."

"I'll stay to answer your questions. But I've also made a copy of Luke's letter for you to keep. I've been in hiding for some time, so I used my time to record Luke's history for others to have.

"Paul mentioned on one of his visits that you were a Roman official in Antioch. When you became a Christian, you were relieved of your duties."

"Dismissed is more like it. But that's given me time to copy Luke's writings. He's a meticulous writer of details. I want to share this with all who'll listen. I plan to travel as far as I can."

Jesse was listening intently and on hearing this jumped up. "I'll go with you!"

Theophilus turned and searched his face.

Judas explained, "This is my impetuous son, Jesse. He doesn't mean to interrupt." The glare he gave Jesse spoke clearly.

"No, no. It's okay," Theophilus replied, "God's Spirit led me here for a purpose. Perhaps Jesse is part of that."

All were silent then, even Jesse who continued to gaze at Theophilus.

Dori stepped forward. "For now we'll find a place for you to rest after your journey. Come, we'll serve some refreshment and then show you your bed."

* * *

Later that evening Theophilus opened the scroll and began to read Luke's letter. Eyes and ears were turned to him as he recounted how Jesus appeared to His disciples during the forty days after the crucifixion. Then he read of His ascending to heaven with the promise on His lips of the coming of His Spirit. Theophilus read until the sun set, rubbed his eyes and spoke solemnly, "We can continue tomorrow, when there's more light."

Judas said, "Of course. You must be weary. We're so excited to have you with us."

Judas dismissed the group with, "The Lord bless you and keep you; the Lord make his face shine on you and be gracious to you; the Lord lift His countenance on you and give you peace."

But Judas and Dori found it hard to find peace.

"Dori, what do you think? Is Jesse to go with Theophilus. What's God telling you?"

"I think we both know. Jesse agreed with the elders, when they discussed his calling, to wait until he had someone to travel with. Now he has Theophilus."

"Yes, but oh, how we'll miss Jesse. God's been so faithful to protect us, and I know He'll protect Jesse, but my heart is heavy. He's truly become dear to me."

Dori replied, "The good thing is: Theophilus is a Roman Gentile, and so traveling with him would be quite safe. A Jewish boy on his own is another thing. Theophilus knows many people and could open doors that Jesse on his own could not."

"You're right. So, if Jesse feels God's leading, we shouldn't stand in his way. This will certainly increase our prayer life. Come, maybe we can sleep now."

*   *   *

The next day Judas called together the people to hear more of Luke's letter.

"Theophilus, please continue. We want to hear what Jeshua told His disciples those last days."

"Of course. Those last words hold much promise. First, He told them to not leave Jerusalem because, as John baptized with water, in like manner, they would be baptized with the Holy Spirit. But this you know. Those who are believers know the Holy Spirit is living within them."

"Yes, we know His Spirit has come upon us."

"I can see that. But the disciples then asked the Lord if He was going to restore the kingdom to Israel—basically defeat Rome. His answer was not what they wanted to hear. He said they were not to know the time, that only the Father knows when. So, then He continued to tell them what was imminent, the coming of His Spirit."

"But didn't He promise to return?"

"Yes. As He finished speaking, two men in white robes appeared, He was lifted up, and a cloud took Him out of their sight. But the men told them, 'This Jeshua, who was taken up from you into heaven, will come in the same way as you saw Him go into heaven.' "

One of the newcomers shouted, "But we've heard He's returned already!"

"Sadly, those rumors abound," Theophilus said, "There was one warrior named Theudas who claimed to be messiah, but the Romans cut off his head and carried it throughout Jerusalem mocking the Jews and Christians. And there was Menahem who entered Jerusalem dressed as a king, but again the Romans killed him. Alas, many have been led astray by these false Messiahs. Men like these are why the Roman soldiers have slaughtered so many Jews and Christians. They see them as rebellious enemies."

After several minutes of silence Judas added, "The Lord warned us. He said false messiahs would come. Now we see it is so."

"True, but He will return. For now, we're to be led by the Spirit who will guide us as we go into all the world to share His good news."

Jesse stood beside Theophilus. "And speaking of that, Theophilus and I have decided it's time to 'go into all the world.' We plan to leave next week. We ask for your prayers."

"And you have them, my son."

Judas embraced Jesse and gathered Theophilus in

his fatherly hug.

* * *

The next week came all too soon. The families in the Garden circled Theophilus and Jesse as they prepared to leave. Judas spoke up, "We shed tears . . . sad because you are leaving, but joyful because you'll be sharing the Words of our LORD."

Theophilus said, "We know we're in God's hands. We're excited to share with Jews and Gentiles the good news of the Savior. We'll leave Luke's writings with you, and (God willing) we'll return to share what we learn of the churches."

Prayers and tears were shed by all as Theophilus and Jesse headed north over the mountains toward Antioch. Dori and Judas watched until they were out of sight.

"Come, Judas, we have food to prepare for the evening meal. I need to stay busy or I'll never stop crying."

"Indeed, my love, we've much to do, right here where God has placed us."

Chapter Sixteen

Psalm 61:1-3 "Hear my cry, oh God, listen to my prayer...Lead me to the rock that is higher than I; for Thou art my refuge, a strong tower against the enemy."

Near the Garden

Hosea and Matthew were on a mission. Meat was needed for the Garden community.

"Matthew, what a beautiful day. And we get to be out in God's awesome creation!"

"It's good to get away. I love the community God has provided, but I do like to get away where it's quiet. Just look at the mountains."

"Let's hope we can find some game. I'd like some meat with my veggies."

"Hosea, what is this I hear of you and Miriam? It is true? Are you getting married?"

"Yes, we're betrothed and will marry as soon as our house is completed."

"I'm happy for you. She loves the Lord and is so good with children. My sister, Naomi, loves her."

"She's good with kids. I pray God blesses us with many."

As they climbed higher they spotted a deer munching on a bush. It was unaware of their presence. Hosea and Matthew readied their arrows and crept closer. In unison they shot their arrows and the animal fell. They quickly gutted the deer and began to quarter it for carrying back to the Garden. They wrapped it in cloth to keep flies away, and with big grins began the trek home.

As they neared the bottom of the mountain they heard voices and quickly hid in some brush. They unloaded the meat and waited.

"Where are you taking us, Peter? We can't walk much farther."

"Quit complaining! We'll be safe in the mountains. The soldiers quit following, but we must hide. We don't want to meet up with robbers."

"But the children are tired. We have to rest. Ever since we left Galilee we've been moving so fast. Surely we can stop soon."

"Okay, let's go over there and make camp. The brush will help hide us."

As the family came toward where Hosea and Matthew were hiding, they looked at each other. What should they do?

Suddenly Hosea's quiet voice could be heard amidst the bushes, "Peace be unto you. Don't be afraid."

The family stopped. Martha gathered her children to her and Peter stood in front of them not knowing whose voice came from the bushes.

Slowly Hosea and Matthew stood.

"You're safe. We'll not hurt you. I am Hosea and this is Matthew. We're just here hunting and on our way home. Do you need shelter?"

"Oh yes! Praise God. You're not soldiers. I am Peter. This is my wife, Martha. We've been running for days. Jerusalem is besieged and the temple destroyed. After Titus came to Judea everything changed."

"You're safe now. Come with us. We're of the Way, Christians."

"We are also! Oh, God is so good."

"Come, we'll take you to the Garden. We're just returning with some fresh meat."

"Please, let me help, Hosea. You've quite a load."

Approaching the Garden, the men and children met them and were excited to see them carrying a load.

"Looks like you were successful," Judas said.

"Yes, Father, and we also found Peter and Martha and their children. They were fleeing to the mountains and have news. This is my father, Judas of Damascus."

"Come. Welcome to the Garden. We'll get your family fed and settled and then you can tell us the news."

The news was not good.

"Titus arrived with many soldiers. Jerusalem and the temple are destroyed. It was awful, so many killed. We heard one group fled to Masada, but I don't know what happened there. We've been running for days. A soldier has been following us, but we've not seen him for a day or so."

"Well, you're safe now. God has protected us and blessed us. You and your family are welcome to stay here."

"Thank you. We're so weary, but perhaps our journey is over."

Chapter Seventeen

Luke 6:27-28 "...Love your enemies, do good to those who hate you, bless those who curse you, pray for those who abuse you."

Near the Garden

The day was crisp and cool. The men trekked to the hills to hunt. As they approached a small valley, Andrew spotted a horse, munching on grass.

"How strange is that," he whispered. "Only Roman soldiers have horses."

The men immediately stopped, knowing the rider must be nearby. Nathaniel ordered the men to spread out and circle the area.

"Be very careful. This looks like a soldier's horse and may be the one searching for our new arrivals."

Andrew spotted blood in the brush and warned Nathaniel. They stopped and at first heard nothing, then a small groan. They carefully approached the bush. There he was.

"Andrew, help me stop this bleeding. There. Hold pressure. Look at his leg. It's definitely broken. We need to straighten it to move him."

They called the other two men to help. As they held the man down, Nathaniel straightened the leg, covering his mouth as he screamed in pain, and then he passed out.

"Get some heavy branches, as straight as possible. We need to keep his leg from moving. Tear off some strips from his shirt to tie the limbs in place."

"Nathaniel, how did you learn to do this?" Andrew asked.

"Before we left Jerusalem, I watched doctors work on others who were beaten and left for dead. I've not had to use that knowledge until now."

"I think our God has a sense of humor, Nathaniel. You learned this while treating those beaten by

Roman soldiers. Now you're treating a Roman soldier!"

"But he wasn't beaten. I think he fell from his horse. Regardless, we need to get him back to the Garden."

"Is that wise?"

"He'll die if we leave him. What do you think our Lord would have us do?"

"Right. The four of us can carry him and lead his horse. This isn't the kind of hunting result we'd planned."

*   *   *

Judas and Hosea spotted the group as they approached.

"What have you found, Nathaniel?"

"I believe this is the Roman that the new family was fleeing from. It looks like he fell from his horse and broke his leg. I want Sarah to look at how I set it. She is better at this than I, and he's lost a lot of blood. Not sure he'll live."

"Call Sarah, Hosea, and let's use a separate room for this man. I think his presence will frighten some of the others."

"Judas."

"Yes, Andrew. What is it?"

"It just came to me now. He looked so familiar. I met him on my way to Damascus. It's been awhile, but I think it's him. His name is Julius. He was curious about God. I'd like to help take care of him."

"Certainly. I'm sure Sarah will need some help."

Dori approached.

"Oh, Dori, you've heard. Is a room ready?"

"Yes, and Sarah's there getting a bed and cloths ready."

"Good. Let's get him settled and let the others know. We need to pray for wisdom and healing."

*   *   *

For several days Sarah and Andrew changed

bandages, applied herbs to the wound and cool wet cloths to Julius's forehead. He had a fever and didn't awaken. Then finally on the eighth day he groaned and tried to sit up.

"Lie back down, Julius. You've been ill."

"Who are you, woman? How do you know my name?"

"I am Sarah. Our men found you nearby. You were thrown from your horse and broke your leg."

Andrew heard voices and entered the room.

"And who are you?"

"I am Andrew, Julius. Do you remember me? We traveled in the caravan leaving Jerusalem on the way to Damascus several months ago. We talked."

"Yes, I think I do. But where am I?"

"You're safe. We found you bleeding and feverish and brought you here. Sarah's been taking good care of you. I imagine you have many questions, but now that you're awake, you should take some broth."

"Thank you, I think. I'm so tired."

"You're weak, sir. But I believe you're over the

worst. The infection had us worried. But we prayed and God was good. You are healing."

"What is this place?"

"After you rest more, we'll talk, Julius. Call me if you need something. I'll be in the next room with Sarah."

Andrew called the elders together to discuss what to do next. A Roman soldier in the midst of all the newly settled refugees could be a problem.

Then Judas and Hosea decided to call a meeting with everyone. Rumors had already spread about a man who was hurt. The meeting included not only the men but also many of the curious women who stood ready to hear the news.

Judas said, "Hosea and I have called you together to tell you about our visitor. He was found by a hunting party over a week ago. He'd been thrown from his horse, broke his right leg and was bleeding."

Immediately murmuring filled the room.

Finally, one of the men shouted, "A horse and

rider can mean only one thing!"

"Yes, you're right. He's a Roman soldier. His name is Julius. Andrew is acquainted with him. They spoke several months ago when Andrew was traveling to Damascus. But the important thing is, if we'd left him in the hills, he would've died."

"But he's a Roman soldier, probably looking for us to kill us."

"He isn't going to hurt anyone. He can't even stand yet."

"But he can't stay here. He'll bring others and our families will be in danger."

"Please, just listen. Do I need to remind you of what the Lord taught us in the story of the good Samaritan? We're not to leave someone, even our enemy, on the road to die. Andrew and Sarah have been talking with him and caring for him. We've seen over and over what God's love can do to change a man. We need to pray for him. Pray that God will change his heart. Can you do that?"

Many heads nodded while voices whispered,

"Yes."

Gideon spoke up, "Let's give him a chance. God may change his heart as He did mine."

*   *   *

It was several days before Julius was able to put any weight on his leg. Sarah had fashioned a crutch from a sturdy limb, but walking was still difficult. Andrew walked with him when he left the room and wandered outside. Most of the community was busy with gardening, cooking, sewing, building or making furniture. Most of the children were doing studies in the community building. When Andrew and Julius entered the building it was quiet, except for one of the elders who was reading from a scroll. They were reading about a Centurion who had sent for Jeshua to heal his son who was ill. Then a tall man went to the front of the group and told how he, a Roman soldier, also trusted Jeshua as his Messiah.

"What does he mean 'Messiah'?" whispered

Julius.

"Let's go outside and I'll explain."

"Was that man really a Roman soldier? How did he come to be here?"

"Let's talk about your first question. We believe that we're all sinners, we all do things that are wrong. Would you agree with that?"

"Of course, we all do things that are wrong, but what does that have to do with it?"

"Everything. God knows we do many things that are wrong, but He is a holy God and wants us to be holy. So, the only way to take away our sin, our wrongs, was to send His Son, Jeshua, to be our sacrifice, our Messiah or Savior."

"Is this the man I heard about that was crucified by the Romans a few years ago?"

"Yes, but He was God's Son and rose again and is now in heaven with God our Father."

"I've heard those stories also . . . the soldiers believe his body was stolen."

"It wasn't. Many saw Him after He arose,

hundreds. You can't make up something like that."

"So, who is that man who claims to be a Roman soldier?"

"He was a Roman soldier. He became a believer in Jeshua. Jeshua teaches us that all life is precious, even a wounded enemy's life like yours. Unfortunately, he witnessed the mass killing of many Jews and Christians and knew he could no longer be a part of that killing. So, he left being a soldier."

"Amazing, to leave like that. He could be executed if caught."

"Yes, he knows that. But his faith in the one true God is more important to him. Come, let's get you back to your room. I think you've walked far enough for your first day out."

* * *

In the days that followed, Julius continued to ask questions.

"Where did all these people come from? How can Jews and Greeks and Romans all live together? How do you survive in this place?"

Andrew patiently answered, "Jeshua taught us to love one another, to even love and pray for our enemies. So when we do that, there is no longer Jew or Greek, slave or free, soldier or carpenter. God has brought this community together. Each person has a skill and purpose for being here. Just as our bodies have varied parts with different purposes, God has brought this varied group together to work together for Him."

"But how? How can this work without a commander?"

"Oh, we have a Commander. God is our commander. But He rules with love and asks us to walk in love."

Julius just shook his head. "I don't understand how love works. I know how things work when there are rules, authority, punishment when someone doesn't follow orders. That works—not love!"

Andrew nodded. "Yes, I can see this is hard for you to understand. But it comes down to choice. We've chosen to walk with God, follow His rules and love one another. You'll have to make that choice also."

Judas had been listening nearby and came forward. "What Andrew says is true. We'll not force you to stay, but if God is speaking to your heart, we'd welcome you as a brother."

"I'm a Roman soldier. This may be working for you, but this is not my place."

"You're free to leave. We ask only that you leave in peace."

Julius hesitated and finally answered, "You saved my life. You've been only kind as I've healed. I'll not bring soldiers here. I can see there is no rebellion here."

"Thank you, Julius. That's all we can ask."

The next morning Julius rode away on his horse with enough supplies to reach his regiment.

Andrew asked, "Do you think he'll keep his word

and not reveal our location?"

"That's in God's hands now. You've shared God's truth. Now it's time for God to work in him."

Chapter Eighteen

"Trust in the LORD with all your heart and lean not on your own understanding. In all your ways acknowledge Him and He will direct your path."
Prov. 3:5-6

The Garden

Judas needed to get out in the sunshine. The fatigue of the last few days had kept him inside too long. He spent an hour in the chickpea field weeding. And then the pain came. His arm ached and it was hard to breathe.

I can't make it back to the house. Guess I'll sit here a bit.

As he closed his eyes the darkness came.

An hour later Leah and Orpah were walking in the field. Orpah spotted a figure lying at the end of the row.

"Leah, it's Judas! We need help getting him home. Stay with him and I'll run and get the men."

"Go. I'll stay with him."

In minutes four of the community men came with a blanket. They placed Judas in the middle and grabbed the four corners. As soon as they arrived, Dori led them to his bed. By now Judas was rousing.

"Oh, Dori, what's happened?"

"Leah and Orpah found you in the chickpea field. You were unconscious. Judas, what happened?"

"Not sure. I had pain in my chest and arm, so I decided to sit down. The next thing I knew I was here."

"You shouldn't have gone out alone. How are you feeling now?"

"I'm okay. I just need to rest."

"I'm worried about you. You work too hard. You aren't so young anymore."

"Dori, my love, I have lived a wonderful, long life. I've been blessed with a loving wife, two God-fearing sons, and many dear friends. And most of all, I know the Messiah."

"Oh, Judas, I'm not ready to let you go."

"I'm here, not gone yet."

The next day Nathaniel and his boys returned from a trip to Caesarea Philippi. The political situation had quieted enough the men felt a trip for supplies would be safe. Garden residents surrounded the wagon as they unloaded some much-needed staples and materials. The men carried off the lumber and building supplies while the women passed out cloth and cooking utensils.

As Nathaniel slowly stepped down, he immediately went to Dori and Judas and handed them a small scroll.

Surprised, Jesse asked, "What is this?"

"Open it. You'll see."

Judas broke the seal and turned to Dori, "Let's go inside. The wind and dust may damage the message."

Once inside Dori said, "Judas, open it!"

"I am. I am."

Tears filled Judas's eyes as he recognized Jesse's familiar script.

Jesse, a follower of our Lord and Messiah, with Theophilus to Abba and Eema and the saints in the Garden.

Grace and peace from God our Father Who sent His Son, our Messiah.

We are presently in Philippi sharing with all who will listen. And thanks be to God, He leads us to many who now have received forgiveness in Christ our Savior. The church here is thriving. Theophilus repeatedly shares Luke's letters and they are received well.

God willing, we will go next to Corinth. I am excited to go there.

We pray for you always, that God may grant you to be strengthened by His Spirit, and rooted in love you may understand the depth of love of Our Father.

I miss the fellowship there in the Garden but seek daily to follow God's leading.

This letter comes that you may know how I am and what I am doing as God's servant. I hold you in my heart.   Jesse

"Judas, he is well. Praise God."

"Indeed. What a blessing this is. We need to share it with the others."

That night as Dori and Judas lay down, Judas whispered, "I can rest in peace now. God's work will continue through both our boys. Hosea and Jesse are His servants, each in his own way. Dori, God has always reminded me, 'Trust in the Lord with all your heart, and lean not on your own understanding. In all your ways acknowledge Him and He will direct your path.' Praise God, He has certainly done just that!"

Kay Penny Eaves is a retired teacher who enjoys Bible study and studying the history of Israel. She has traveled widely and lives in Montana. Her travel and living abroad several years widened her horizons and believes God has used that dramatically in her life and writing.

Made in the USA
Lexington, KY
25 May 2018